To my dear nephew Archer. You are going places!
– With love, Uncle Eric

For my mom, who always believed in me.
– Kent

Kane Miller, A Division of EDC Publishing

Text copyright © Eric Ode 2014
Illustrations copyright © Kent Culotta 2014

For information contact:
Kane Miller, A Division of EDC Publishing
PO Box 470663
Tulsa, OK 74147-0663
www.kanemiller.com
www.usbornebooksandmore.com
www.edcpub.com

Library of Congress Control Number: 2013953405
Manufactured by Regent Publishing Services, Hong Kong
Printed May 2020 in ShenZhen, Guangdong, China

Paperback ISBN: 978-1-61067-287-0

Busy Trucks on the Go

Kane Miller
A DIVISION OF EDC PUBLISHING

Drivers honk to say hello.
Busy trucks are on the go,
building bridges, fixing roads,
lifting big and heavy loads.
Town to town and here to there,
busy trucks are everywhere.

Here's a truck that's loud and big.
Excavator loves to dig.
Next is dump truck, large and strong.
Watch him move that dirt along.

Concrete mixer roars and rumbles.
See his drum? It turns and tumbles.
Soon he opens up his spout.
All the concrete rushes out.

Hear him rumble. Watch him run.
Big bulldozer gets things done.
Scooping rocks and dirt and sand,
here he comes to lend a hand.

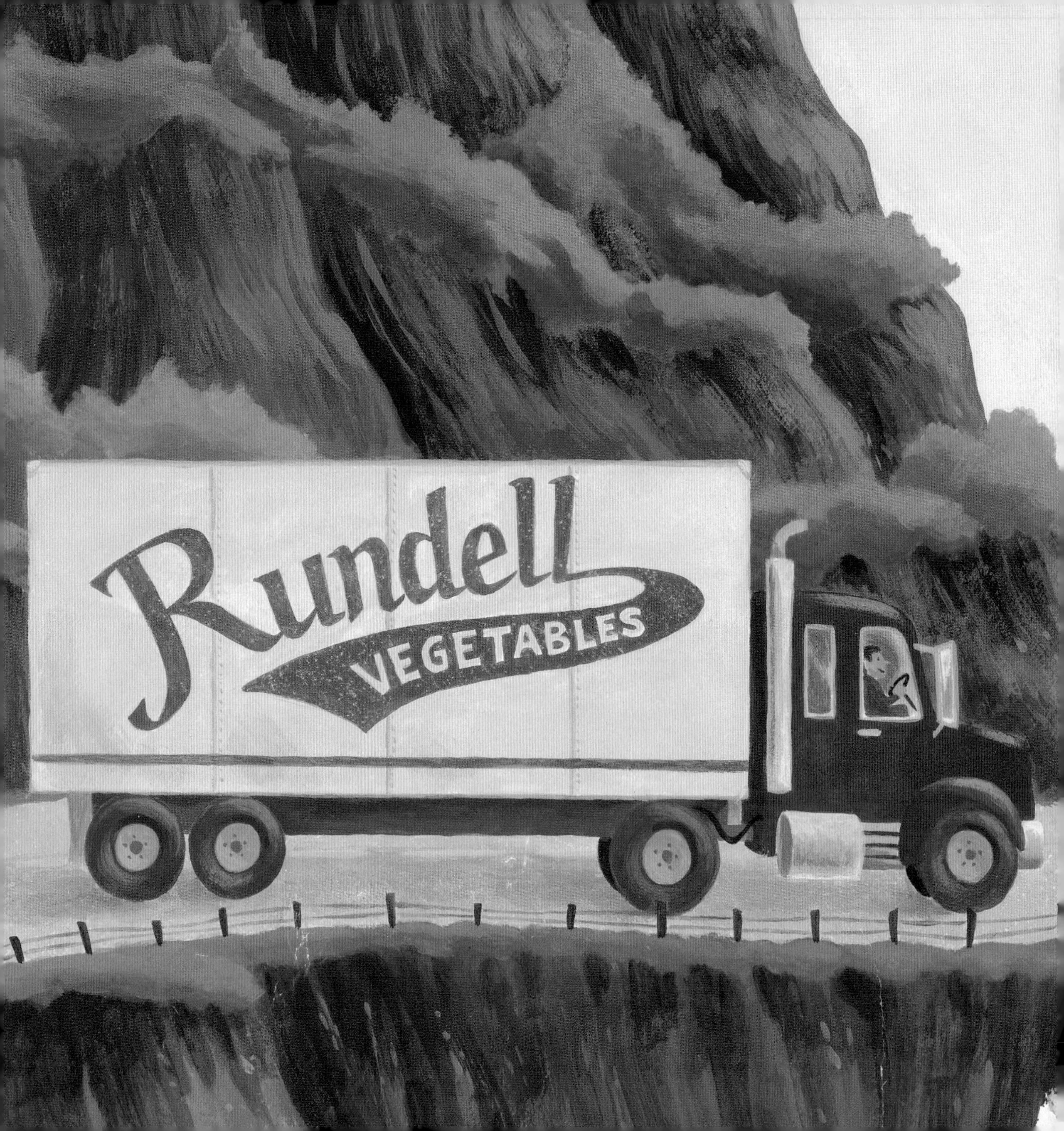
Rundell
VEGETABLES

Freight trucks carry clocks and cakes,
books and boots and garden rakes.
Through the mountains, up and down,
there they go from town to town.

What a busy farm today.
Tractor pulls a load of hay.
Later he will till the rows
where the corn and cabbage grows.

Here's a car that cannot go.
Who will give this car a tow?
Who will come to save the day?
Mighty tow truck's on the way!

Mail truck stops at homes and stores,
bringing letters to their doors.

School is starting. Climb inside!
School bus gives the kids a ride.

Fire trucks have work to do.
Move aside, and let them through.

If there is a fire about,
pumper truck will put it out.
Is there someone hurt or stuck?
Here comes paramedic truck!

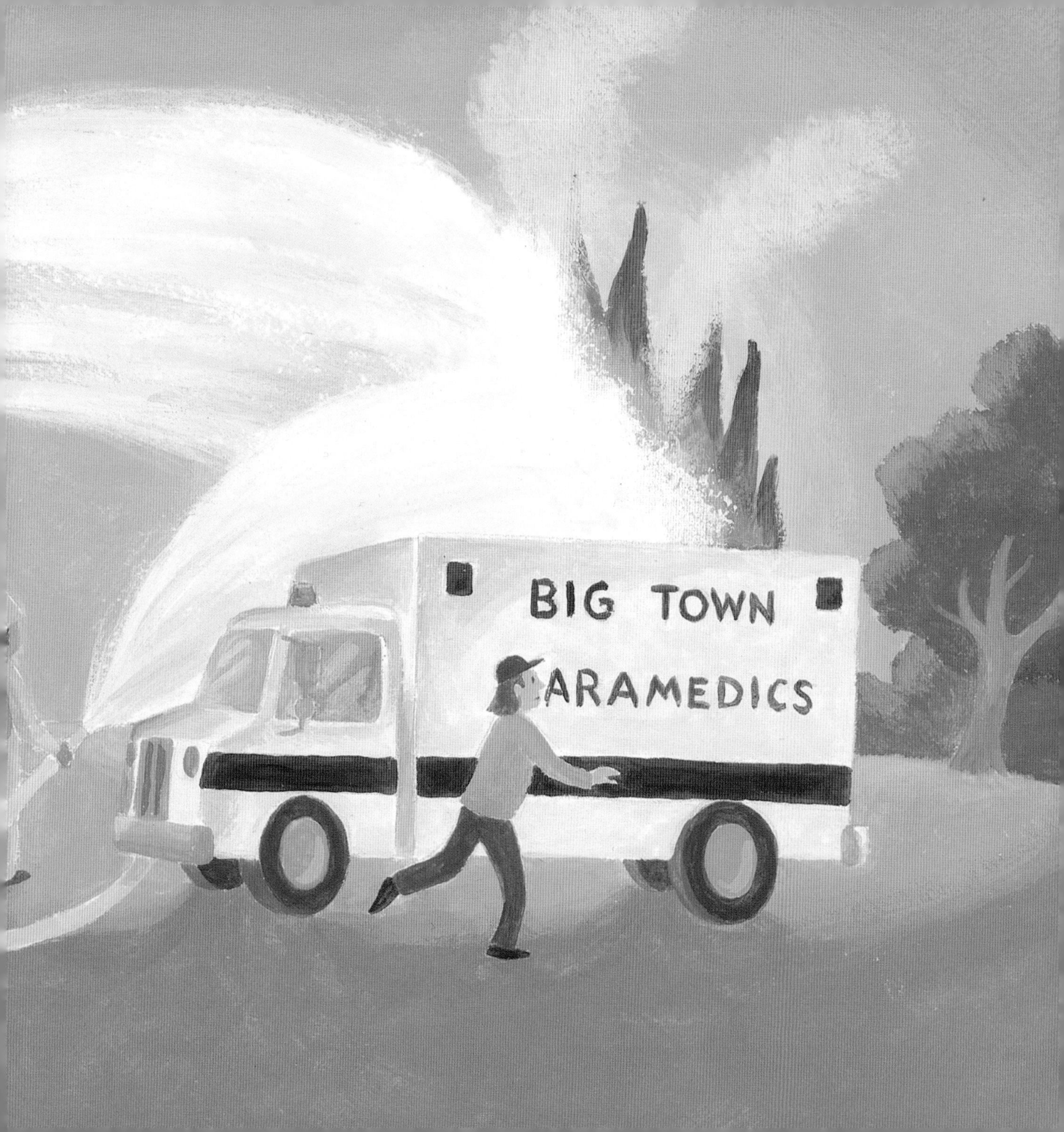
BIG TOWN
ARAMEDICS

Rumble, rattle, clatter, crash!
Garbage truck collects the trash.
Up and down from street to street.
Soon the town is clean and neat.

Now recycle truck is here.
Watch those papers disappear.
Cans and bottles; boxes, too.
One day they'll be something new.

City bus makes many stops,
bringing folks to stores and shops.

Who's this busy truck we meet
cleaning up the city street?
Big street sweeper's right on time,
scrubbing off the gunk and grime.

Now it's time to stop and rest.
Busy trucks have done their best.
Moon and stars are shining bright.
Busy trucks will say good night.